The Bull
in the Forest

PETER ZACHARY COHEN

Drawings by Ruth Bornschlegel

4906

Atheneum   1969   New York

for my father
CHARLES A. COHEN
who did some underwriting

The Bull
in the Forest

one

IN THE CHILL, vague starlight the bull rested. He was used to the dark woods, crowding tall and jagged around the edges of each open pasture. The bull was tall and dark and jagged, too.

He noticed the brown bear come out from among the trees and push under the pasture fence, where the wires crossed a gully that was narrow but steep.

In warm times, when grass was full and the raspberry bushes were heavy in the open places, the bull had always quietly eyed the bear, and had always seen the bear squinting back at him, while the thick, hairy arms kept sweeping the berrybushes past the narrow, sharp-toothed mouth. Now the days were cool and the nights long again; grass no longer grew fresh each day, and the bushes were thin, scraggly, and empty. Two young, fall calves were in the pasture.

The bull snorted; he put his horns low and pawed up the ground with his front legs. The bear stopped at the edge of the fruitless bushes, then rose up on his hind legs and showed his sharp teeth with a grunting snarl.

The bull slowly stomped forward, the dry, autumn dust smoking up around him in the dim and silent starlight. The bear shook his head and cut the air with his teeth. He held ready the long claws of his giant forearms. The bull kept stomping forward, and snorting, his breath blowing puffs out of the smoky dust.

The bear swung down on all fours and began loping away. The bull charged, and the bear plunged back through the gully and on into the forest. The bull stopped immediately, and as the dust was settling he rested again. The bull wasn't angry and he wasn't excited. He was used to the bear.

He was used to the harsh, grinding, chainsaw whines the forest often made when the sky grew bright; but this morning, when the sun came back, the world brightened quietly. And there was none of the sharp, hunting-rifle bangs that he sometimes heard in these short days of the cooling season. It didn't matter. The bull was used to silence, too, and as the long morning shadows began to shrink back from the pasture, and the gray frost began to melt and sparkle, the bull carefully watched for the men to come again, riding the machine piled high with loose, dry, sweet grasses.

The bull had grown used to the men, who walked upright like bears but were smaller, and he was used to the machine, and he was used to the horses that were like strange, wrong-smelling cows. The horses also stayed in the pasture, and always came to eat the hay without bothering the cows and calves very much.

It was only if he saw men on horses that the bull became fidgety. He'd learned that men on horses meant he was going to have to go some-where—but *where*? It had always been annoyingly hard to know what men on horses were up to.

He'd tried charging the men on horses, but they'd never loped away like the bear; they'd always dodged and come at him again with ropes and points and whips, until he'd gone through one open gate or another, and then abruptly they'd let him alone.

So the bull stayed alert. He watched carefully, till the men and the machine had come and gone, leaving the horses behind. Now he strode steadily forward, mumbling deep in his throat, slowly swinging his heavy head and horns from side to side, clearing a space for himself to eat at the hay. Gradually the bull had gotten used to his life: he ate what grass or hay or grain he could find; he tried to keep cows and calves within his reach; he swatted off insects, chased the bear, ran from men on horses, and all was well. He paid no attention to other things—not the occasional airplanes passing high overhead, nor the farm machinery he sometimes saw beyond the fences, nor any noises the forest made. He barely glanced at the birds and mice that were now scuttling near him, taking bits and bites of feed. When he was full, he calmly ambled away, his stout tail lightly flicking, to relax by himself as usual near the forest edge.

Suddenly a hard pain stabbed him high through one shoulder. And he didn't understand it.

He didn't connect the pain with the familiar, sharp, hunting-rifle bang a part of the forest had just made. He snorted harshly and looked quickly around for the points and ropes and whips of the men on horses. He didn't like being taken unawares.

There was no one there.

But every time he moved, the pain bit harder in his shoulder.

And there was no one there.

He pawed and snorted, and felt sharper pain. He went hurrying to find an open gate and every time he moved the pain bit harder. He went bellowing and storming all about the pasture. All the cows and calves and both horses galloped out of his way. But the pain kept stabbing, and every gate was closed. He knew all the gates; they were all closed.

When he'd gone through gates before, other pains had stopped.

The bull stopped. The pain kept up. The bull began to quiver with pain and rage. The

pain would not quit and the gates would not open and he couldn't find any men on horses. He was not used to this. He wouldn't put up with it longer! He went at the nearest gate, head down. The fence wires for a quarter mile on either side of him shook and twanged. The sharp barbs cut into his head and legs, and the cuts smarted with the pain; but the twanging stopped, and the gate was twisted junk, and the bull was loose in the forest.

two

A MAN RAN through the forest. His red jacket
and soft, red cap flickered among the trees.

He had been moving very slowly. He had
seen the fresh track of a bear and had cautiously tried to find where the bear had gone.
He had seen something dark and heavy moving out in a wide clearing, and right away he
had raised his rifle and shot. Then he'd seen
his mistake.

He kept running back deeper into the forest. Branches whipped and snapped against his
face and clothing.

But he'd come hunting with two friends,
and they had heard the shot and then the bel-

lowings, and the friend who was closest came running through the woods, to see if the man needed help. The friend wore a long, tan coat that fluttered with red handkerchiefs pinned to it, so other hunters could see him.

The bull broke through the woods into a small, stony clearing, just as a fluttering man came hurrying out of the woods at him. The man was without a horse, but was carrying a stick. The bull wanted no more sharp points jabbed in his shoulders, and charged instantly.

This man dropped his stick and sprang up a tree. It was the first time the bull had seen a man do that, but it didn't ease the pain.

"Wild bull! Wild bull!" the man in the tree shouted loudly. The bull scarcely heard the sounds—men always shouted at him when they were making him move. He pounded across the clearing and on through the woods again, taking narrow passages where he could or smashing his way forward through brush and young trees, trying to find where to go, where the pain would stop.

He came onto an old logging trail and went headlong through the tall dry grasses that smelled like an unused farm lane. He didn't

slow up for the white birch tree that was dead and fallen against another tree across the lane. When the bull struck to push it aside, too, a blast of solid wood hit him; his ears rang, the world spun, lights flared everywhere. The bull lay on the ground. His head was so aching and dizzy that the bullet pain in his shoulders was numb. It felt good to lie down. So the bull lay still, and didn't feel the injured shoulder muscles begin to stiffen. He didn't know that soon he wouldn't be able to move enough to get up.

His running had kept the wound loose and openly bleeding, so now the flies began settling, and buzzed and bit and tickled. Many, many, and still more, flickering and droning, stinging flies. Violently the bull heaved up on his feet, whipping his sides with his tail. He floundered over the top of the birch trunk and ranged farther along the logging trail, chest-deep in stiff forest grass.

Somewhere in the woods near him more shots sounded, quickly, one after another. The bull paid them no mind and kept on going. Amid the tall grasses ahead of him the bull heard something coming, then smelled the bear; he smelled the bear before he saw him.

The bear burst at him out of the grasses but didn't rise up or snarl. The bear swerved and leapt pell-mell into the woods, his short tail tucked tight behind; he crashed invisibly away.

The bull kept going through the tall grass grown up in the old logging road. The grassy lane met another one, a dark, dusty lane, curving out from under woods too thick and shady for any grass to grow. Running around the curve of the dusty lane, came another man with a stick. The man was only half-visible in the shadows. He skidded to a stop and clamped the stick to his shoulder.

The bull stopped and looked. The bull tried with his aching head to figure what to do. The man stood and stared back. Then the man suddenly jumped and waved and cried out, "G'wan, g'wan! I'm after a bear."

The words meant nothing. Men always shouted at him. But he could drive off a walking man with a stick. The bull dipped his head and attacked, lunging out of the tall grass and onto the shaded, dusty lane.

This man in front of him yelled again, and dove among the trees. The bull thundered on, keeping to the smooth and dusty trail.

"Mad bull! Mad bull!" The man was yelling and running behind him now.

But he was outrunning the man. The torn muscles were limbered again, the blow on the head from charging the tree trunk still partially numbed the pain, few flies could pester while he moved so fast. The bull kept going. The man's voice grew dimmer behind, then quiet.

The shaded lane opened out onto a small, hilly meadow, where the grasses were shorter and softer and smelled like pasture. The pain was almost gone. This must be the pasture he was being chased to. The bull slowed down. He felt very hungry and glad to get there. He lowered his head and began to graze.

three

BELOW ONE of the meadow hills was a tent, and near the tent a boy was kneeling, busy beside a stream that was trickling toward a small lake. The boy's arms were still too short to steady and aim a heavy rifle, and the only way he could be out on a bear-hunting trip with his father and his father's friends was to do the chores. He didn't mind doing chores for a hunting camp, yet washing pans and plates got boring and he looked around often. He saw the bull.

The boy's father was a lawyer, and they lived in town; but the boy had school friends who lived on farms, and he had visited them.

The boy knew that bulls usually didn't belong deep in the woods. He guessed by the way the bull stepped while slowly grazing that he was lame or hurt. So the boy didn't think to be afraid. He went into the tent and came out with a clean pot full of oatmeal and walked up the hill to give it to the bull.

The bull immediately looked at him and began to remember the way men brought feed when the coolness became cold, and heavy snow covered all the grass. The bull smelled the oatmeal and came interestedly closer. Suddenly the bull threw up his head and swung half about. The quick, hard jump sent bolts of pain shearing down his legs, and the sound he'd heard behind him became a man stumbling out onto the meadow, wildly waving his arms, and still trying to yell but mostly just loudly gasping, "Look out! Mad bull!"

The bull saw again the man's waving stick. The bull got angry at being given no peace. He snorted and pawed. The pawing brought more pain. The bull bellowed, and though the boy had stopped several paces away, the bull's roar thundered around his ears.

The boy slowly let the pot of meal sink and

drop, as he began retreating.

In a moment the bull started after him, moving away from the stick, following the small man with the grain.

The boy started to run; he raced along. He heard the hoofs galloping behind him and knew he couldn't reach the trees; he ran for the tent and quickly decided not to jump inside it. He dove around its corner as the bull's horns caught one of the guy ropes. Screeching and ripping, the tent, with everything in it,

sprang after the bull. The bull dodged and fought in panic, jerking the tent into the stream where it caught among some rocks; ropes snapped and the bull escaped on into more forest, where pains kept jabbing him.

The boy stayed lying flat in the open where he had been left. He heard the man who had yelled come running and stumbling closer and sink down, puffing too much by now to utter a word.

four

THE BOY pushed himself up on shaking knees and began focusing on all the torn and scattered equipment soaking in the stream.

"You all right?" the man puffed at him. He was a heavy man, bulky in a dark red-and-black coat. Before this hunt, the boy had scarcely ever seen him in anything but pure white. The man was his family's dentist.

"I'm fine. I feel fine," said the boy quickly.

"Scared, though, I'll tell you. You're white as milk."

"No! I'm not scared. I'm not." the boy exclaimed. He couldn't be scared, or hurt. He couldn't be in the way at all.

"Sure you're scared," bellowed the dark and heavy man—his dentist. "What's the point of it, if you're not scared? What's the use of getting chased by a mad bull if you don't get the thrill of it?" The man's voice kept roaring. "You're all confused, boy. You're supposed to just tend camp, not to be fearless." Then the man laughed as loudly as he had spoken. It was the same everything's-all-right talk he made in his office, though in his office he'd always been very calm and quiet.

Suddenly the man stopped laughing; he began digging cartridges out of a pocket. "Say, we ought to shoot a warning signal to the others. And that bull might come back. I'd better load this gun."

"Wasn't it loaded before?" the boy gasped.

"Emptied it at a bear. Didn't you hear all the shooting? That *bear heard me*. Ran like a rabbit. Then this bull came at me. The whole wood's turned into a bull. Magic. Witches' doings, I tell you." Again the dentist shook and boomed with laughter.

The boy didn't understand. His father'd kept telling him before he came that he'd have to remember to be quiet, keep quiet, stay *quiet.*

Then, quickly, the boy jumped up; his job was to keep the camp in order. All at once he saw here was a chance to show how good a job he could do. He hurried to rescue all the equipment from the stream.

Soon, he was building the campfire back up and reheating the lunch-time cocoa. His father, draped in the long, tan coat with its patchwork of pinned-on handkerchiefs, was standing near him, still breathing hard from a long run. The dentist was sitting and listening, looking weighted down by his heavy, black-and-red coat. His father's other hunting friend was resting down on one knee. He was a smaller man, who owned the hardware store beneath the dentist's office, in the town where the boy lived, some thirty miles away. He'd come dressed in a bright red jacket and cap, but now his cap was missing. His face and hands had scratches on them as red as his jacket, and even though he was talking, his eyes kept looking up and around at the woods circling the meadow.

". . . so I just plain took off running," the smaller man kept saying. "I don't know why it charged me. Suddenly there was this bull, head down and bellowing right at me—"

"Just the way it happened to me!" exclaimed the dentist.

"I shot to save myself," said the hardware store man. "Then it ran into the brush. I didn't know where it'd come out of next. So I took off running."

"It came out on a clearing and took after me," said the boy's father.

"Sure gets around, doesn't he," laughed the dentist.

The hardware store man answered sharply, "This isn't a joke. We've got to get bullets into that bull before it hurts somebody."

"Did your shot hit him?" said the boy's father.

"Sure," was the answer. Then the man stopped: "Maybe not," he said. "It happened so sudden, how could I tell?"

The boy's father said, "Well, if he's shot, and we don't hound him, and if he's like other animals I've known, he'll soon lie down and stiffen up on the ground. If he's just riled,

he'll forget about it quicker, if we leave him alone."

"Why should he forget about it?" said the dentist. He pointed at all the strewn equipment. "That's probably a beautiful memory for him."

The boy felt a puff of laughter fill his cheeks, and he held it back, but it was a funny way to think of it.

His father just said solemnly, "If there's real danger we ought to go back after the sheriff—form a posse for morning. Someone around here will probably be missing a bull. We'll find out who owns him; maybe someone who can handle him."

"Handle him!" screamed the hardware store man. "This'll handle him!" he exclaimed, holding up his rifle. "I'm telling you, that bull's dangerous. Attacked me without my doing anything. I got in one shot to save myself."

"Never could afford to go hunt African buffalo," said the dentist. "Maybe this'll be just as good."

"We came to hunt bear," said the boy's father. His voice had become very clipped and clear: "Not just to kill the first thing in our way."

"But this is an emergency," said the dentist.

The hardware store man jumped to his feet, the long scratches stretching across his face. "This is to save somebody else's kid! Who maybe won't have a tent to save him!" The man's eyes glared, and the scratches on his cheek made him look like an Indian in warpaint. "Most of the timber around here still belongs to the county. It's public land. *Anyone's* liable to be wandering through here on a weekend like this, if they know about the place. We've got to shoot up that bull now! It's dangerous, or it wouldn't be out running loose!"

"Listen," said the boy's father, "when I grew up on my granddaddy's farm, we patched an awful lot of fence we'd thought was cow-proof. When any critter that big wants to go wandering, it just goes. We ought to find out who owns it and get some help."

"You're just being a spoilsport," said the dentist. "You want to bring a whole mob of other guys through our hunting ground."

"A trigger-happy bunch of possemen in

here'd be more dangerous than the bull!"
snapped the hardware store man.

The boy had to just keep stirring cocoa and
listening to his father being argued at by his
friends. He wanted to speak up, too, because
he wanted to be part of the hunting camp;
because he'd brought oatmeal to the bull and
then had had to run for his life. What fun
that would be to talk about now!

He realized that apparently the dentist
hadn't seen him drop the meal pot. He
wanted to tell them how the bull was lame,
and hungry enough to sniff toward a meal pot,
and that it was probably just the dentist's
shouting when he'd run out of the woods,
that had frightened it, and that they probably
shouldn't start trying to kill it. But he didn't
dare. He'd visited farms enough to have ideas
about animals, but not often enough to be
confident about his ideas now. These men
towered over him. He knew he couldn't speak
as big and sure as they could. They'd think
he was just too young and dumb to be with
them. He couldn't get up courage enough to
interfere.

"Okay, you may be right," he heard his

father say. "Let's go try to find the animal now."

The men gulped down the hot cocoa and hurriedly checked the workings of their rifles and the matches and flashlights they carried in case they got lost.

"That trail of broken brush is going to be plain enough," said the dentist.

"We'll get rid of that menace," said the hardware store man. "Farmers ought to keep their bulls penned in."

The boy right away put out the fire and went and climbed into a tree, to wait out of danger, as his father decided he should.

five

AT FIRST the bull had fought ferociously on through the timber, fighting to get rid of the big thing that had leaped at him, not realizing the tent ropes had snapped and that it was only brush and branches clawing at him as he pushed by.

He had to pause, finally, when he came to the edge of a low, round bog. But the stirred-up pain in his shoulder kept throbbing. The forest stood thick behind him, and a haze of clump brush in front. The bull wasn't used to such an overgrown, grassless place. Mosquitoes and flies began collecting about him, especially on his wound and the cuts made by the fence. The bull snorted his annoyance and shambled on around the bog.

The floor of the forest became steeply wrinkled. The bull had to struggle along narrow, winding, tree-cluttered ridges, for he sensed that walking through the bogs below would be even harder and slower. And he had to keep moving—go somewhere.

The ridges all led uphill, until the forest opened again. The bull looked out across a narrow valley to where a wide hillside was glowing yellow in the late afternoon sunlight. The land sloping downward right in front of him was thick with low bramble, but the breeze brought the scent of soft grasses. Over there, across the valley, must be the pasture where the pain would stop and he would be left alone. The bull had started down to cross through the line of red willow stems and dark green grasses that choked the bottom of the valley when he smelled a new scent.

A sharp sneeze came from among the willows. In front of him, a huge head poked above the stems, and made another sharp sound. The bull saw a gigantic horse with wide, flat horns stepping out toward him. The

horse had no rider, so the bull kept walking closer, moving toward the grassy slope. The bull had never seen a bull moose before.

Nor had the moose ever seen a cattle bull. The moose was strong after a good summer and was ready to begin finding a mate. With that on his mind, the moose had no welcome for other animals intruding into his territory.

The bull saw the moose stand and paw up clouds of dust with quick, hard movements. Long legs made the moose nearly twice as tall as the bull, and the broad, jagged antlers blotted out half the hill slope behind him.

The bull started to paw, but pain stabbed him. It made him shiver a moment, for he had been steadily losing strength, both through the bleeding wound and through running and tramping in the forest. The bull stopped pawing and snapped air out sharply through his nostrils. He stood and lowered and shook his horns, warning the moose away from his new pasture. But he saw the giant antlers come charging at him, close above flashing legs. Dark and drumming like a cloudburst.

Quickly the bull braced on his hind legs to try to lunge his great weight forward.

Jolting and skidding, the moose went to one side and hauled up in a bigger cloud of dust. The bull saw the moose's head perked high above the dust, heard the moose snort with a questioning kind of bark.

The bull grunted deeply. Then he made a step toward the moose, shaking his horns more threateningly, not knowing it was the scent of the oozing blood on his shoulder that was stopping the moose, for strange blood meant wolves as wolves meant blood.

The bull saw the moose prance this way and that, with quick up-and-down steps, and then swing about and go crashing back among the willows and dark grasses where he disappeared.

The bull was used to other animals acting that way. He gave forth a bellow of triumph and ownership, a gushing roar that soared out from his low, stretched throat; then he began to barge on through the narrow valley bottom to take control of the pasture beyond. The dark grasses in the bottom felt stiff and coarse. The red willow stems among them were tall; and, right away, as he pushed into them, the world became all dark-striped and damp smell-

ing, and lost all solidness. The bull's heavy
legs mired in the spongy soil where the longer,
thinner legs of the moose had traveled in and
out.

The more the bull tried to struggle ahead,
the more sharply the bullet wound tore at him
and the more he stuck. The short way ahead
to the open, grassy slope became endless. Insects were swarming all about him. A wild,
volcanic bellow erupted once and then again
and again. The bull's whole aching body was
in it.

*The branch of the tree had gotten harder
and narrower. The mosquitoes had found him.
The boy kept looking down at the equipment
that lay in soaked bundles on the meadow,
because the men had come rushing back before he'd had time to spread them. He had
come on the hunt to keep the camp, and now
his father had told him to stay in the tree. But
he was cramped and pestered in the tree. He
wanted to show how good a camp he could
keep.*

The time passed slowly, endlessly; yet the

afternoon shadows kept pushing steadily and quietly out from the western edge of the meadow, toward darkness. Everything was quiet except the mosquitoes. Finally he jumped down, ran out on the meadow, and began spreading things to dry. But they would dry better on a clothesline. So he got some rope free—then the forest roared, and roared again, and again; it was a bellowing that came up from the ground, or out from the trees, or out of the air. The boy released the rope and ran back to the tree.

six

FINALLY the bull tried to back out of the slough mud, but managed only to wallow around sideways, and remained caught.

He looked up through the grasses and willow stems, and saw another figure, standing tall and dark beyond the edge. It was the bear, up on his hind feet. The bear was slowly shaking his head, as he always did when he was curious or threatening to fight.

The bear's round stomach was puffing in and out with heavy breathing, for he had run a long way through the forest since he'd been frightened and stung by loud noises from a running man. The skimming bullet had left an ugly cut from a hip to a shoulder, and knots of flies were settling on the bear, too.

The bull shook his horns at the standing bear, as he was used to doing, and the bear dropped down on all fours—but stayed in a crouch, teeth showing in a silent snarl.

The bull watched as the bear began to prowl back and forth, swiftly crouching down low, then lifting up and prowling, beginning to make a steady muttering sound.

The bull was used to charging with the bear so close. He struggled and struggled to charge at the bear. He ached and floundered tiredly. He roared out in deep, raw bursts. He lost the feel of the aching of his shoulders. He was getting so coated with mud that there was no place left for the flies to bother him.

The bear had no such protection. The bear was pestered and tired, hurt and hungry; food was scarce and dry now in the forest and he wanted to sink his teeth deep into the meat of the bull's shoulder if he could get to it. The bear tried to stalk around behind the bull, but drew his paw back from the sinking touch of the mud. Instead he went directly toward the bull.

The bull saw the bear crouch down. The legs bunched beneath the round, furry body, and then the bear slowly stretched forward his big front paws.

Slowly the bear's paws came through the grasses and willow stems. The bull shook his horns, maddeningly unable to charge; he felt the claws gently scrape and hook about his horns. Suddenly the bull's neck was jolted, and then stretched and strained and the bull squirmed and writhed to resist, but only succeeded in swimming, swimming in the mud, and being dragged a little way toward the bear's grunting mouth.

The bear let go and sat back, his stomach puffing in and out, as he caught his breath with soft whistling sounds. Then slowly he reached forward again.

Again the bull's neck was jolted, again he swam forward a few inches in the mud, bending down willow stems and matted grass in front of him, until the bear again sat back panting and whistling.

Now the bull was close enough for the bear to clamp his big forearms completely around the horns—but when the bear moved again he silently swung one paw murderously at the side of the bull's head. The bent willow stems intercepted part of the blow, and the bull, watching closely, got his horns around and caught the paw on one tip. The bear jumped back, screeching and then grumbling fiercely. The paw stung worse than the bullet scrape along his back, and the bear grew meaner because of it. But he was going to have to get the bull closer, and get around behind.

The bear reached slowly and quietly, and again the bull had his neck jolted and strained till it felt as if it were nearly coming apart. The bull thrashed about angrily with his legs and wounded shoulders, bellowing without realizing; and his front hoofs found solid dirt. The bull shoved himself forward and felt fresh pain stab and tear through his shoulders and he bellowed savagely as he staggered immediately but shakily up out of the mud.

The bear rolled silently away from him, then came swiftly back up on all fours, teeth showing, but with his breath hissing very heavily.

"Where is it?" muttered the hardware store man. All around him he could see only dizzying ranks and stripes of trees, thick trunks and thin trunks, dark-colored and light-colored, straight trees and bent trees, and here and there dead trees lying crossways that had to be climbed over, or crept under, or walked way around. Between all the trees was the spindly brush, dying and drooping toward winter. The noises had echoed from everywhere.

"Too bad he quit trying to tear the woods apart," said the dentist. "We could've found him quick."

"It's almost too dark now to find footprints," said the boy's father.

"I'll bet it's just kept up this ridge," said the hardware store man. "C'mon, let's keep close."

"Wait," said the boy's father. "Let's listen a bit. We make so much noise ourselves getting through this timber we can't hear straight."

"No! Let's get this job done," the hardware store man insisted. "It's bound to have gone up this ridge."

"I vote to listen," said the dentist. "It might save us some walking—or running."

The dark red-and-black checks on his heavy coat stayed still and strangely square among the tree trunks and brush. The pinned red handkerchiefs hung limply now around the boy's father, like autumn leaves on a tall, tan shrub. The bright red jacket glimmered in the deepening shade, and shivered restlessly.

seven

BOTH ANIMALS eyed each other, as they often had. Both were too tired to make the next move. The grassy slope across the slough was being colored a berry purple by the beginning sunset, and the cold of a north woods autumn night was starting to clear the air of insects.

As the sky darkened, the bear quietly ambled off to one side, then in an instant he came pouncing back.

The bull's mud coating blunted the claws, but nevertheless a paw crashed heavily against his side and more pain shot through his shoulders as he stumbled about to keep from falling over.

The bear dodged silently from side to side, then in close and away; he swung his paws, trying to knock the heavy bull down, to make him helpless. The bull staggered sideways; his hind legs tangled, and he sat down but jerked himself back up. Pain burned in his shoulders. The bull had forgotten all about men with sticks—he blamed all his pains on the bear. Finally he moved just before the bear did, just before he saw with certainty which way the bear was jumping. He had known the bear a long time and he guessed well. In one movement he ripped the bear's side with his horn tip, across the long cut left by the hunter's bullet.

The bear leaped and screeched, then snarled in fury. And right afterward the bear stood up on his hind feet and faced toward the forest, leaving his back exposed to the bull. The bull lowered his horns, but was too worn down to take his advantage. Before he could get himself going into a lunge, his duller nose smelled what the wild bear had smelled quicker, and then he saw the gray forms at the timber's edge.

The faint scent of blood in the forest, the

bellowings, the growls and screeches of battle, all had promised a winner and a loser; and the wolves had come for the loser, or both.

Instinctively, the two big animals came together. They were hurt and weary; they knew it, as the wolves knew it. The bear started toward the forest, moving up the brambled slope, and the bull went beside him; the bull remembered driving dogs away from his pastures before. The wolves milled about, staring hungrily, but uncertain of how to begin, one by one they had to step aside, until the bull walked with the bear into the thick timber and seemed to be escaping. Then several wolves sprang at them from behind. The

bear spun like a whirlwind, slamming with his claws; other wolves came dashing through the woods, trying to drive them back into the open. The bull tiredly lowered and swung his horns and the wolves snarled but jumped away from the sharp points.

The bear spun back around and as the two went walking ahead other wolves leaped out of the underbrush, and the thick-furred bear or the heavy bull crowded and squeezed them against the close timber, so that the wolves squirmed and limped away, and grew more cautious.

The wolves formed a low, gray circle, like a moving ring of deadly toadstools that flowed through the darkening forest. The bull plodded slowly forward, going back down the timbered ridges. The bear held to the bull's pace, each half-shielding the other, and the fresh blood from the bear's horn wound kept drawing the wolves along.

The wolves stayed silent in their gray, flickering circle. The bull had time to feel a slow, twisting fever-sickness begin in his stomach and enlarge; his ears and nose and shoulders and feet began to tingle numbly.

His eyes had to strain dizzily, constantly trying to stay awake and alert.

The bull began to slow down, and the wolves came spurting in from their circle, charging up the ridge sides. The bear once again began turning and walloping with his forearms. The bull had to remember to lower and wave his horns, or to stumble a little sideways, crushing wolves against the trees.

The night air was becoming icier. It was hardening the gray coating of mud on the bull. It was helping slow the blood from the bear's fresh wounds, and it thinned the scent. More and more wolves grew hungrier, and silently drifted off after other, less battle-ready game.

Soon after that the bear, whose wounds were not deep, recovered all his strength. But he had no more interest in trying to attack the jagged bull, and he no longer needed the bull's protection. The bear grew bored with the bull. Suddenly the bear stopped; he stayed for a second motionless in the starless darkness below the trees, his nose twitching. Then he drove to one side in a long bound, and a large bird burst from the brush and flustered

upward to a limb. The grouse tried to pause
there a moment, but the bear didn't pause.
He leaped high in the darkness. The limb
broke sharply and loudly as he struck it; the
grouse tried to rise farther, but a thick arm
was swinging past and the grouse squawked
and fell with the bear.

Immediately the bear rose up from the
ground, snarling and growling. The bear
shook his head and held his claws ready, warning the bull away from his food.

The grouse meant nothing to the bull.

The bull kept on hobbling back through
the thick and unfamiliar forest alone.

eight

THE BOY sat near the softly crackling fire, seeing its light glowing roughly on the men's faces
and shining in thin sparkles from the long,
smooth rifles. But the fire was making only a
little orange-red hole in the cold night. The
small lake close behind him was in darkness.
The miles of forest around them were black
and silent. Stars glittered quietly in the round
patch of clear, dark sky above him. This
wasn't a ballfield where all the excitement
died just because it was empty, or when the
lights were turned out. This was a hunting
camp, and the boy wanted never to be left
home again.

". . . we could've stayed out longer," the hardware store man was saying. The firelight darkened his scratches. "It ought to be dead, not wandering loose out there."

"We'd have been shooting or bellowing at each other, if we'd hunted till it got any dimmer," the boy's father said.

The boy wanted to tell them how the noises here had been so strange he'd had to run back to the tree; but he wasn't supposed to have been out of the tree. He couldn't get his voice feeling loud and strong enough inside him.

"What makes you think we're safe now?" the hardware store man said. "It's charged the tent once already."

"That's just 'cause it was chasing after the boy," said the dentist.

The boy kept still by the fire. He'd promised his father he wouldn't get in the way. His tongue was scraping sourly in his mouth, for the supper he'd given out was a shapeless batch of food they were eating cold out of the cans; but it wasn't his fault—he'd had to spend all his time in the tree. He wanted to remind them it wasn't his fault about the tent, either. It was still lying sprawled about when they got back. But he didn't know what they'd say to him if he spoke.

"At least you heard its noises," said the hardware store man. "You know it just plain charged me. I had to shoot to save myself."

"We better know; it charged us, too," said the dentist.

It was lame and hurt, the boy thought. The more he'd sat, worrying and wondering alone in the tree, the more he'd remembered it that way. The bull had charged when the dentist had run out so frighteningly.

The dentist grinned at the man in the bright red jacket: "But fast as it charged us, I don't think your shooting did much good."

"Where's that bear *you* were shooting at?" the hardware store man answered sharply.

"I wonder," said the boy's father, quickly and mildly, "if it wasn't really a wounded bear we were listening to. Those sounds didn't make clear sense. Maybe it's something we ought to try and figure out."

"It was his bull and my bear," joked the dentist, "and they've fallen down a tin well."

"That bull was just bellowing with its head to the ground to make its sound spread," said

the hardware store man. "It's crazy smart. We've got to get rid of it before someone else comes near it."

It was bellowing because it was hurt, the boy decided. Maybe now it was hurt worse. Suddenly he figured: maybe it needs help. It would've eaten some meal; he was sure of it! The men ought to know how the bull acted. He felt himself getting strong enough to try to speak out. . . .

Suddenly the hardware store man ex-claimed: "Hey! I see it now!"

The boy tensed, his back went icy as he spun around trying to see quick just where, which way to run; again he saw the huge, black, thundering charge . . . He was just remembering the huge shape and beating hoofs. He was seeing only the quiet darkness.

"That bull's got hydrophobia. Just like a mad dog," the hardware store man breathed, without moving. "That's what it is. Bulls can get it, too, you know."

The boy sank back, quietly shaking with relief. The man was only thinking. The boy heard the others settling back also.

"Well, at least a bull won't bite us," chuckled the dentist, and then let out a deep, relaxing sigh.

"Hydrophobia's no joke," the boy's father said. "It gets in the throat. That could be the reason for those strange noises."

The boy stayed small by the fire. He wouldn't trust his voice. What would the men say now if he'd told them he'd gone on purpose toward the bull to feed it?

But it hadn't been frothing at the mouth; it'd been calm, and it'd looked like it would've eaten some meal. Did that make a difference? He didn't know how to ask. He didn't dare.

"Looks like a trip to the sheriff, after all," said the dentist.

"We better not," the boy's father said now. "Not till we're sure. Lots of people might hear about it and get overscared. Then who knows what they'd do? They might start needlessly killing things. We've got no choice but to run that bull out the first thing tomorrow."

"And shoot it down before we get close to it," said the hardware store man. "We can't take chances. I've already had to shoot when it charged me."

"So I've heard," said the dentist, and he stood up and stretched wearily. "We'll need our sleep," he said. "I'll bet we have some pretty dreams."

The others stood up, too, their rifles shimmering as they moved. The red handkerchiefs pinned to the boy's father's coat now danced in the flickering firelight.

The boy looked down at the food cans all speckled with light. He'd dug a garbage pit when they'd first pitched camp yesterday, to keep smells and hungry animals from bothering the camp. He ought to take these freshly opened cans to the pit, but his father said, "Here, better let me tonight."

"I'm not scared," said the boy.

"I know you're not," his father said quietly.

"Do you think the bull's out there?"

"No, not here. Not now."

"Then why can't I take it? It's my job."

"It's just from not being sure," his father said.

The other two men began talking about their bedrolls that were still too wet to be comfortable.

The boy knew he could have had them all completely dry, but he'd had to stay hiding in the tree, swatting mosquitoes, then shivering in the evening chill, alone and wondering. He wanted to remind them, but was afraid it'd sound like complaining.

Now the men were deciding to keep the fire going all night. But he hadn't had time to gather enough firewood from the woods, which were now pitch black.

So he helped them carry water from the lake to put the fire completely out.

The boy was angry at the way the camp was going on around him. He knew he could keep a good camp, he could help in lots of ways, if only things would let him. But he wasn't going to just stand there asking to do things and trying to make excuses for what he hadn't done, and he didn't know how to explain what he knew about the bull.

Maybe if he could talk to his father alone—
but his father came back and his father's
friends were constantly right there. They were
all moving in and out around the tent that
they had put back up, still ripped and sagging,
nearer the lake and far from the way the bull
had taken across the stream and into the
woods. The boy simply kept doing what he
was told.

Soon he lay curled down inside his own wet
sleeping bag. But he couldn't sleep. He
squirmed about a long time with his thoughts.
He worried about the bull, and about his
father who was going to hunt it tomorrow and
might be attacked by it again. Was the bull
mad, or just lame and frightened by the
hunters? Was it hurt? Did it need help? Would
it be best to leave it alone? Would it be *safe*
to leave it alone? How could *he* tell? He remembered the meal pot, still lying out where
he'd let it drop.

He'd need the meal pot to have a hot breakfast ready in the morning, and he'd have to
start cooking it before daybreak. That he
knew. He knew there was enough wood left
to do that. And he was going to have a good

breakfast ready. He was going to keep on being part of the hunting camp. He wasn't going to let them just work around him and leave him in a tree. No one had told him not to get the meal pot now.

nine

QUIETLY the boy got out of his sleeping bag, eased his bare feet into his boots, and stepped softly out of the ragged tent.

He paused in the icy air. He thought he'd caught the sound of wild bellowing, still rushing through the darkened forest. But as he stood very still he couldn't hear it. Just the same, he felt the beat of his heart quickening and the chill of terrible possibilities creeping in his backbone. He couldn't let himself go quaking back into the tent.

The cooking pot ought to be in camp. He ought to have ·a hot breakfast ready at daybreak.

He wished he could go back inside the tent and sneak out a gun to take with him. If something were close, he wouldn't have to aim it. But what if he saw nothing and the men heard him sneaking with the gun? He shivered at that. And now, standing up and with the fire out, he could see the star reflections on the lake. They twinkled very cheerfully. The stars overhead seemed very familiar and calm. The darkness around him felt cool and asleep. The faint burbling of the stream was a very gentle, steady sound.

Quietly he stepped away from the tent, and gradually he crept into the star stillness and aloneness; he kept stepping across the meadow, nearer to the light whispering of the stream, and soon he was moving past the place where the tent had first stood. Now he stared ahead and low at the ground, looking for the first silver shimmer of metal.

Here he was on his first hunt and the only thing he was getting to hunt was a cooking pot. He tried to laugh about it out loud, like the dentist would have. But the back of his neck only tingled instead, and he felt very serious and unsure.

But he wasn't going to get worried. He didn't look behind him, nor far up to either side. He didn't believe he should have to. Because there would be nothing there. Nothing to be scared of. He wasn't going to be scared of the woods.

Then he saw the ghost looming tall in the darkness in front of him. . . .

Head down, exhausted and lame and fever-sick, the bull was trying to find more oatmeal to lick up. Suddenly he noticed the boy standing near him.

The bull didn't even jerk his head up, but just stared. The small man he saw didn't seem very threatening. The bull started closer to see if there might be more grain with the man. As the bull moved, all the pale patches of dried mud on him shook like the armored skin of a dinosaur.

The bull rattled and shook. The boy thought: *Hydrophobia!* But he didn't turn to run. He knew that was useless, with the tent moved farther away. He couldn't let the bull charge the tent now, anyway. He wished he had some meal with him. And quickly he saw how slowly and awkwardly the shape of the bull was coming; he began hoping that escape wouldn't be necessary. The bull was too lame, too hurt-looking. But the boy couldn't keep himself standing still. He felt himself slowly backing up. He made step after slow, even, backward step, and watched the bull keep following him. He dared not make any sudden movement—until suddenly he found he was back within an arm's reach of the tent.

Then the boy stopped, and the bull stopped and tried to understand the camp: the tent, the strong smell of men and of wet ashes, and the fainter scent of gun oil. Nothing looked like a feed bunker; nothing smelled of grain.

There was the lake. The bull had drunk when he had recrossed the stream, yet the fever from his wounds was raising his thirst again. The boy watched as the bull hobbled slowly around the edge of the men-things to the water's edge.

The tent canvas near the boy's arm moved and the man who owned the hardware store came out so abruptly the boy was startled and jumped, though the bull didn't seem to sense it.

The man was startled, too. "What are you doing here?" the man gasped. Then: "I *thought* I'd heard something."

"Couldn't sleep. Sleeping bag's too wet," the boy mumbled.

"Mine's damp, too," the man murmured. "You'll have to dry them out better tomorrow." The man gazed up at the sky and all around; he seemed light as a moth without his bright red jacket. His face was vague and scratchless in the starlight. "Wish it were dawn," the man said, "so we could get after that bull. I keep seeing it in my sleep. The way that lake water glimmers even looks like a bull drinking over there," he pointed. "But of course with hydrophobia they can't drink. Gets in the throat, like you heard. Well, you better come back in and get some more rest, too," the man said, and the boy quickly moved and held the tent flap so the man could go in first. . . .

The bull drank till he could hold no more. Then there was nothing else that seemed good and nothing familiar around him: no cows, no fences. There must be another part to this pasture, where he would feel better.

When the boy quietly poked his head out again soon afterward, the bull was gone, and the boy lay back down feeling more sleepless than before.

Yet he found himself coming awake with his father and the other men, already in the first light of dawn.

ten

THE MEN rapidly and uncomplainingly ate the breakfast he hurriedly made of plain bacon and bread toasted on sticks over a small, quick fire, with only cold canteen water to drink. Then his father and his father's two friends went away toward the stream and into the woods to hunt down the bull.

No one had given him any *special* orders. "You keep yourself safe," his father had said, and as soon as the men were gone and he had hung up the bedrolls to dry, the boy abandoned the rest of his camp chores again. He was sure the men wouldn't find the bull. He had seen in the dawnlight, by looking quickly and carefully for the faint dark trace through the frosty grass, that the bull had gone back the way it had first come.

Now he went away across the meadow, too, and this time he found the meal pot and brought it back. He reloaded it with the last of the box of oatmeal and put the top on it, as carefully as the men had checked their rifles.

He carried it first to the forest gap out of which the dentist had come yelling and start-ling the bull the day before, and there on a dusty lane he found two sets of tracks—the ones coming and those going.

Cradling the pot on one arm, more sure of himself than ever before, the boy followed.

The forest was thick and quiet. The fresh daylight had already turned cloudy, and the sky was dull. The deeper he went down the dusty and darkly shaded trail, the more he began again to be unsure; it felt like he was sinking gradually into the earth. Or into a trap. He heard a swiftly moving rustling off in the trees; he saw a flash of fur: a squirrel.

A lot of noise, but a small squirrel—he felt much better.

The dusty, shaded lane led him out under a long, narrow stretch of the heavy sky, onto an old logging road that was thick with tall grass. Though the air had not warmed much, a few mosquitoes were about, for they had found shelter here. Gullys of bent-down grasses showed where animals had passed through the roadway during the night. The biggest disturbance began where the bull's tracks left the dusty lane, and the boy pushed on through the grasses, following it.

Through the tall grasses and mosquitoes and the noise of his own movements, the boy kept walking, shifting the pot from arm to arm as its bulkiness began bothering him, and then tiring him. Sometimes he swatted at the mosquitoes and sometimes he just endured them. On both sides of him, the thick timber of the forest rose steeply toward the clouds. Ahead he saw a big white birch tree fallen and leaning across the trail.

The bull was alert at the first sounds of the boy's coming. As the rustling sounds and then the scent of the boy came closer, the bull started to turn around, but he'd been unable to clamber over the big log during the night,

and his muscles had stiffened resting against it. The wound in his shoulder was festering and was swollen into a tight pink mound. The bull moved, and his rested brain felt pain as harsh as ever. He jumped from the shock of the pain and snorted sharply.

The boy heard and stood stock-still, unable to see through the grasses.

The jump had stabbed with a hotter pain, and the bull bellowed, a coarse, high-pitched scream.

The boy felt his hands become sweaty against the pot. He felt terribly small, yet his eyes and ears suddenly felt stretched huge and wide; his muscles twitched.

The bull could smell a man and feel sharp points stabbing his shoulder everywhere, but he couldn't see anything. He was paining, and being taken unawares. He raged forward, and the boy heard the jolting of hoofbeats and saw a giant shape darkening at him through the grasses. The boy dropped the pot and turned to get off the lane. He saw only the thick forest tall as night in front of him, as he ducked his head and ran into the many tough, stiff, sharp-needled branches of the crowding trees. He grabbed and pulled on a prickling branch and fought to get into the woods. He heard a thudding crash right behind him; a high, choked bellow smothered him under a flood of noise. The branch snapped away, and the boy tumbled forward into the jabbing and scraping grip of more limbs.

As quickly as he was stopped, he looked up through an array of pine boughs. He felt the ground vibrating; he heard banging and pounding sounds. The banging stayed loud, but steady. The boy hesitated to move. He wondered if he was safe. He listened to the banging. He took a deep breath and moved a little. Vaguely through the trees he saw a sweep of grasses shaking.

He waited and watched. The shaking and sounds seemed to grow milder. He wanted to stay hidden, or sneak off through the trees. But he wasn't sure what had happened. He couldn't be sure what had happened. He wanted to go see.

He got himself to squirm, silently—almost silently, despite the stiff, thick branches—back to the edge of the lane. He found the pot he'd again dropped; the lid was off, but the meal flakes had only partially spilled. So he took the pot and slowly, carefully, stood up, and waited as he began hearing a deep gasping sound, as if steam were now bursting from the ground beneath the grasses. The boy could see nothing else. The sounds stayed where they were.

The boy measured a step away from the trees, and another, always keeping one foot balanced and ready to spring back. He told himself he knew he could get back into the trees, so he made another step through the tall grass, and another, and he found the bull sprawled on the ground.

The boy saw the swelling of the wound, saw the long tongue gasping out from the frothy and dirt-fringed mouth. He saw three of the huge dark legs stroking and digging against the torn ground, but one front leg stayed stiff and still. Gingerly, slowly, the boy tried easing the pot forward.

The bull shook and snorted; the horns slashed from side to side and patches of dried mud flung loose as the bull rolled and heaved, roared and struggled to get up.

The boy dumped the meal on the ground before him and sprang back to the trees and there halted, listening, watching, panting, still holding the emptied pot like a weapon, until he heard what sounded like the bull snuffling for the meal.

Then very quietly the boy worked himself away, gliding, then walking steadily back along the grassy road. He turned off and continued back through the shady, dusty lane, and finally he got back to the meadow. He filled the pot with water from the lake and carefully returned the whole way. Cautiously he approached the bull. . . .

Once more the bull shook and challenged

him but was unable to stand. The boy set the pot down and waited until the bull, growing calmer, arched his thick neck up from the ground in order to reach into the pot to drink.

When the boy started back to the meadow for more water, he heard the grasses ahead of him rustling beneath some heavy movement.

Then he heard his name shouted.

It was his father, and the two friends, who had heard the new bellowings, had found the camp empty, and had discovered all the footprints on the dusty lane.

"Here!" the boy shouted loudly at them. "I've found him!"

He heard a light click, like rifle metal hitting a button or a belt buckle.

"He's hurt and dying!" the boy shouted at them.

eleven

STILL ATTACKED by pain, sick with fever, sur-
rounded by men in a place he wasn't used to,
the bull shook his horns and grew more mad-
dened as he tried to rise and fight but couldn't.
The man in the bright red jacket quickly set
down the water pail and leaped back.

The bull recognized the water scent and
splashed his mouth into it, till his head
drooped again, wearily.

"Do you think he'll make it?" the hardware
store man puffed. He'd already made several
trips from the lake; it was far and the pail
was heavy.

The boy shook his shoulders. He didn't

dare guess. The wound was swollen, and dark, and oozing pale yellow and green water. He kept sweeping away flies with the long branch he'd cut.

Suddenly with a vicious roar something began snapping and whining and tearing behind the bull. But the bull was used to machinery, and only began trying to nuzzle again at the pail, and tipped it over. He didn't see the owner of his pasture, and the dentist, still in his dark and heavy coat, forcing a power saw into the big white tree blocking the old road, so that the farmer's truck behind them could get through. Only at the last moment did the bull see two men stalking silently toward him.

One of the men was shaking strangely. The boy's father had run two miles through the woods to the car, then had driven to find a phone; now, with the red handkerchiefs still pinned loosely to his long coat, he was returning with someone else.

Just at the last minute the bull saw them come down behind him. He stopped sucking at the pail. He held still, tense, watching. He felt their fingers, like flies walking over him.

His skin shivered. The movement hurt him, and they were behind him; he waited, and watched.

Suddenly one of them rose up and came at him with something thin and flashy. Pain sliced through him, and he bawled hoarsely. He heaved to get to his feet, and grunted as he banged his horns against the ground, trying to strike back.

Then he sank weakly down.

But he felt much cooler, and soon the paining and the men and the noises disappeared.

"Will the poor fellow make it?" the hardware store man asked.

The veterinarian shook his head and stood up. "It's too soon to tell."

The chain saw stopped roaring. In a few moments the truck was driven close by.

When the bull awoke, he knew where he was. It was a stall in a barn where he'd stayed before, when cold, wet snow had covered the pasture grass, and where all his feed had always been brought to him by a man with a bucket or a hayfork. He felt calm in the stall. He was used to the stall. He was not surprised

when his food was brought, as he remembered. But other men came also and tightened
stiff, biting ropes around him, and fingered
him and splashed him and jabbed sharp
thorns into him. But then they always loos-
ened the ropes. And he shook at them, and
they left, and he grew stronger in the stall as
new snow fell outside, beyond the familiar
openings; he became able to stand on his feet,
and then to hobble out into the icy yard, and
pack the snow and stand tall and jagged, but
quiet, there.

From the yard he could see the dark green
car that also came once in a while, and the two
men, one smaller than the other, that always
got out to bring him a bucket of grain, and
to stand peacefully and make calm noises at
him for a while.

"I just keep wondering why he ever charged
your friend in the first place," the boy men-
tioned suddenly one day.

"Animals easily get confused," his father
said. "They become frightened or angry when
they needn't be."

"But there was only one shot—at first. What
I mean is—" the boy paused—"I mean—I keep

wondering—how could your friend have shot
him in the *side,* if he was charging?"

His father made a strange kind of smile.
"Sometimes men get confused, too," he murmured.

"I hope *I* never," said the boy.

"Oh, you can hope," said his father, laughing. He shifted his weight against the pole
fence. "I'm still confused why you didn't tell
us right away how calm he was about that
oatmeal."

The boy looked up. "It's hard to explain,"
he said.

Then the days kept growing longer and eventually they also began being warmer again. The bull began to pace restlessly about the yard. The white snow shrank and gurgled and dwindled away over the ground and into the mud, and finally the yard gate was opened and the bull walked with the cows back out onto the pasture. The bull moved with a limp, but he chased after the bear the first spring night that he saw the bear getting too close to the calves. He had gotten used to the limp.

And whenever the boy appeared at a pasture fence, with a bucket, and peacefully called, the bull ambled calmly toward him. It didn't matter that the boy seemed a little bigger than he once was. The bull was used to the boy.